UP!
UP!
UP!
SKYSCRAPER

Anastasia Suen

Illustrated by **Ryan O'Rourke**

Charlesbridge

Text copyright © 2017 by Anastasia Suen
Illustrations copyright © 2017 by Ryan O'Rourke
All rights reserved, including the right of reproduction in whole or in part in any form.
Charlesbridge and colophon are registered trademarks of Charlesbridge Publishing, Inc.

Published by Charlesbridge
85 Main Street
Watertown, MA 02472
(617) 926-0329
www.charlesbridge.com

Library of Congress Cataloging-in-Publication Data
Suen, Anastasia, author.
    Up! up! up! skyscraper/Anastasia Suen; illustrated by Ryan O'Rourke.
        pages cm
    ISBN 978-1-58089-710-5 (reinforced for library use)
    ISBN 978-1-60734-925-9 (ebook)
    ISBN 978-1-60734-926-6 (ebook pdf)
1. Skyscrapers—Design and construction—Juvenile literature.
2. Building—Juvenile literature. 3. Construction equipment—
Juvenile literature. I. O'Rourke, Ryan, illustrator. II. Title.
TH1615.S84 2016
720.483—dc23   2015026832

Printed in China
(hc) 10 9 8 7 6 5 4 3 2 1

Illustrations done in Adobe Photoshop
Display type hand-lettered by Ryan O'Rourke
Text type set in Humper by Typotheticals
Color separations by Colourscan Print Co Pte Ltd, Singapore
Printed by 1010 Printing International Limited in Huizhou, Guangdong, China
Production supervision by Brian G. Walker
Designed by Martha MacLeod Sikkema

To my husband, Cliff, the architect—A. S.

To my kids, Kaylee, Riley, and Liam—R. O.

dirt

bedrock

Flowers

FLORIST

BAK

Dig, dig, dig!
All around
A long thin trench
In the ground

DRILLING RIG

To go up, we must first go down.
We dig a deep trench around
the entire construction site.

trench with rebar

CRANE

When the trench is deep enough, we place steel bars called rebar inside. Now we are ready to make the basement walls.

concrete retaining walls

Pour, pour, pour!
Wet concrete
A line of mixers
Along the street

It takes a lot of concrete to fill a trench. After one mixer empties out, the next one moves up so we can keep pouring.

CONCRETE MIXER

PIPE

HOPPER

RETAINING WALL

retaining walls

dirt pit

EXCAVATOR

After the concrete hardens, we dig out a pit for the foundation. An excavator scoops up the dirt, and dump trucks carry it away.

Dig, dig, dig!
Down, down, down
A giant pit
In the ground

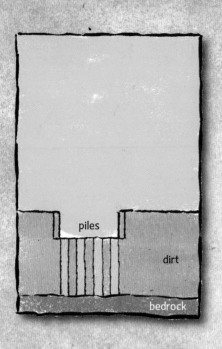

Pound, pound, pound!
Around the block
Pound each pile
Into the rock

PILE DRIVER

Under the dirt is solid rock called
bedrock. We pound long concrete
piles into the bedrock to hold
the building steady.

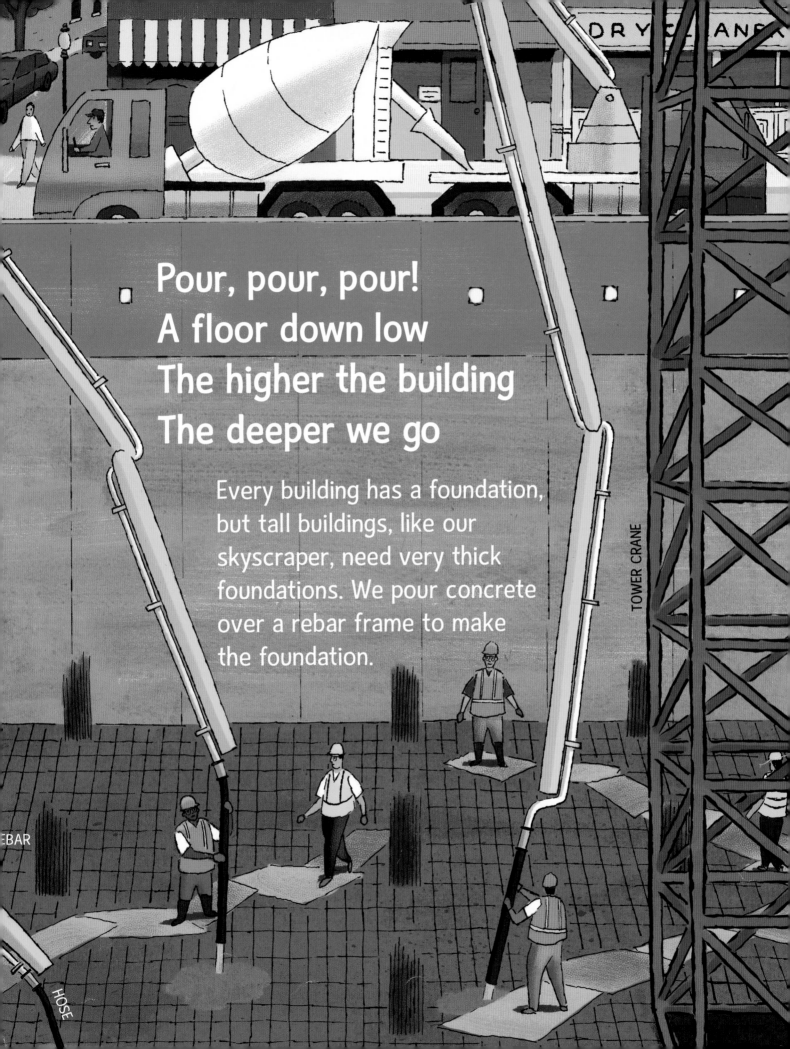

Pour, pour, pour!
A floor down low
The higher the building
The deeper we go

Every building has a foundation, but tall buildings, like our skyscraper, need very thick foundations. We pour concrete over a rebar frame to make the foundation.

TOWER CRANE

REBAR

HOSE

Bolt, bolt, bolt!
Each column down
Bolt it, bolt it
All around

A crane lowers steel columns onto
bolts sticking out of the concrete.
These columns will support the building.

base of
tower crane

columns

COLUMN

BOLT

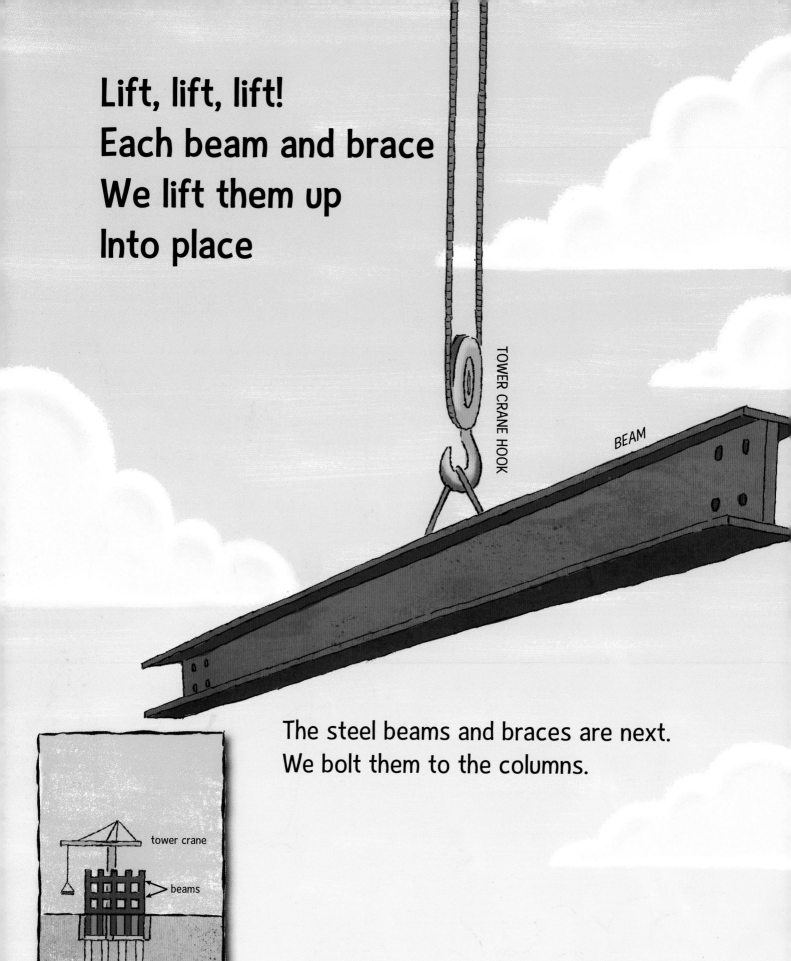

Lift, lift, lift!
Each beam and brace
We lift them up
Into place

TOWER CRANE HOOK

BEAM

The steel beams and braces are next.
We bolt them to the columns.

tower crane

beams

Bolt, bolt, bolt!
Beams and more
We bolt the decking
To make the floor

DECKING

BEAM

tower crane

columns
and beams

CONCRETE
HOSE

CONCRETE
FLOOR
SLAB

We pour concrete on the decking to make
the floor slab. Then we move up to make
the next floor.

Up, up, up!
With a flag and a tree
We're topping off
For all to see

Everyone who works at the job signs
their name on the last beam. We lift it
up in a topping-off ceremony with a flag
and a tree. But we're not done yet!

TOWER CRANE

BEAM

tower crane

columns
and beams

FLOOR SLAB

The wall on the outside of a skyscraper is called a curtain wall. We set metal frames in place by bolting them to the floor slabs. The glass panels fit into the metal frames.

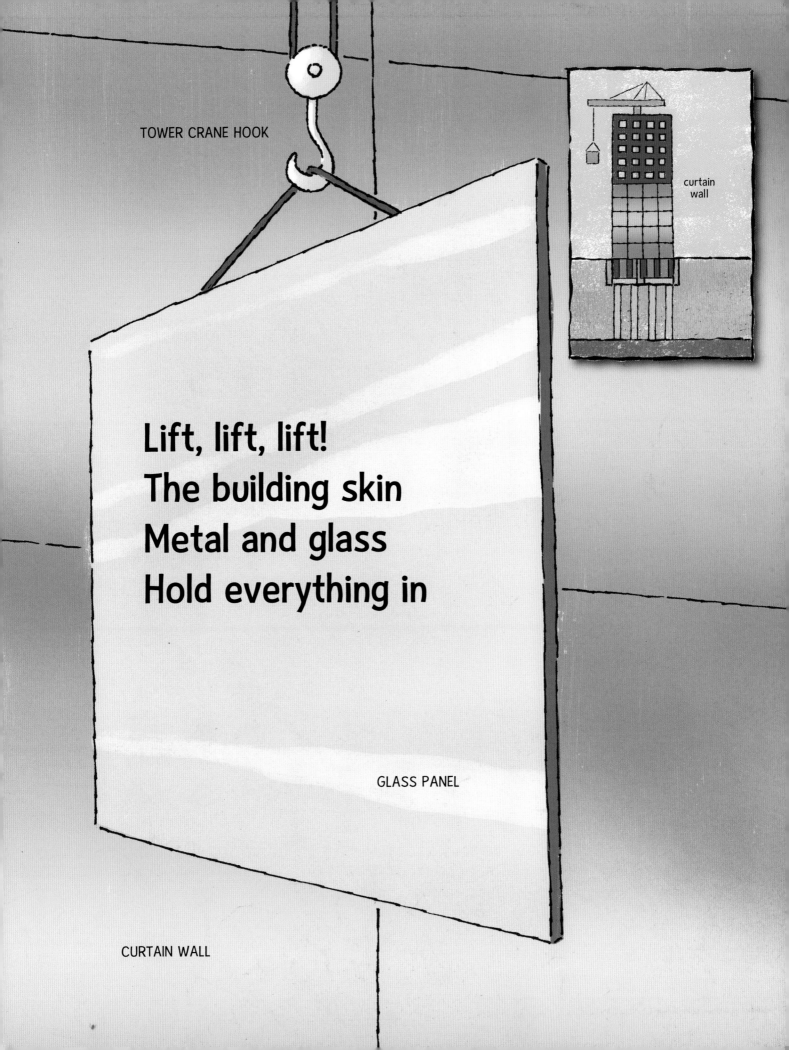

TOWER CRANE HOOK

curtain wall

Lift, lift, lift!
The building skin
Metal and glass
Hold everything in

GLASS PANEL

CURTAIN WALL

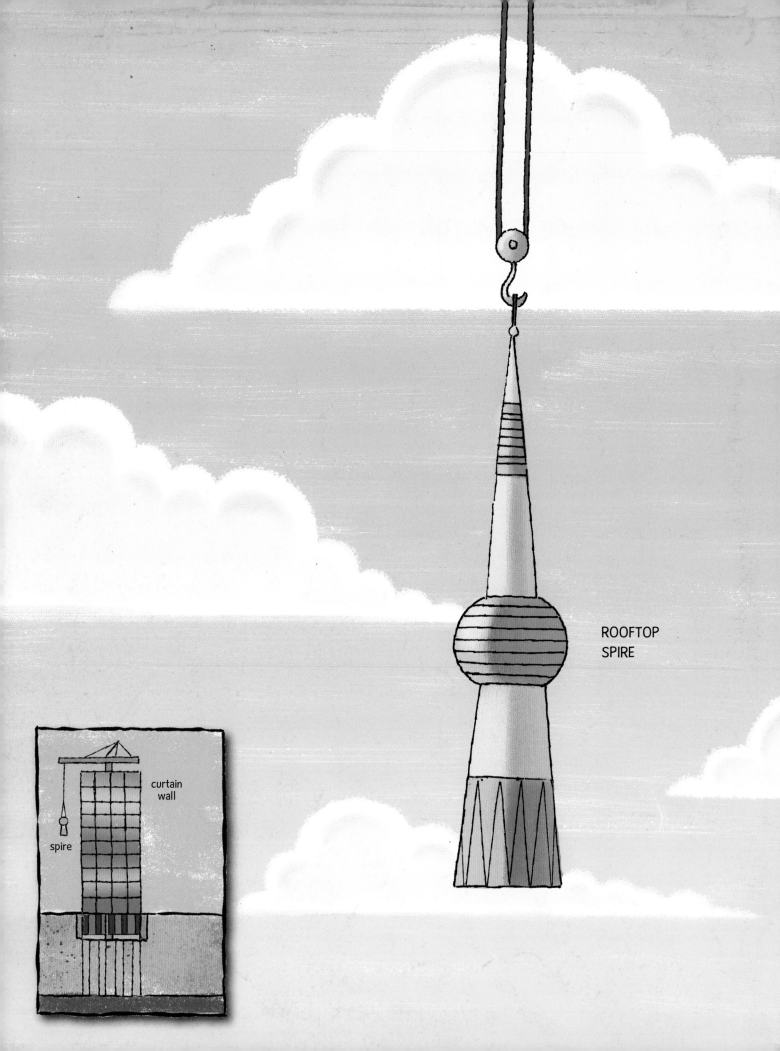

ROOFTOP
SPIRE

curtain
wall

spire

Up, up, up!
We reach the top
We finish the roof
And then we stop—

Skyscraper!